listening

speaking

writing

All in Reading

book one

余光雄
Grover K. H. Yu, PhD
學歷／
美國新墨西哥大學語言教育學博士

國家圖書館出版品預行編目資料

All in Reading book one／余光雄編著.－－初版二
刷.－－臺北市：三民，2009
　　　面；　公分

ISBN 978–957–14–4761–2 （平裝）

1.英語 2.讀本

805.18　　　　　　　　　　　　　　　96014453

© All in Reading book one

編 著 者	余光雄
責任編輯	陳乃賢
版面設計	謝岱均　許嘉諾　曾鐘誼
插畫設計	王孟婷　許珮淨
發 行 人	劉振強
著作財產權人	三民書局股份有限公司
發 行 所	三民書局股份有限公司
	地址　臺北市復興北路386號
	電話　(02)25006600
	郵撥帳號　0009998–5
門 市 部	(復北店) 臺北市復興北路386號
	(重南店) 臺北市重慶南路一段61號
出版日期	初版一刷　2007年8月
	初版二刷　2009年9月
編 號	S 807080

行政院新聞局登記證局版臺業字第○二○○號

ISBN　978-957-14-4761-2　（平裝）

http://www.sanmin.com.tw　三民網路書店

序

　　「閱讀」在學習外（英）語的過程中佔極重要的角色。「閱讀」可說是最方便、最直接且最常用的英語學習途徑。因此，閱讀教材的好壞會直接影響到學習效果。坊間雖然有很多進口的英文教材，但由於不是針對技術學院學生及高職或綜合高中的學生編寫，以至於唸英文變成一種痛苦與折磨，教師在實際教學時也有不便之處。尤其在固定的進度壓力下，授課時數又有限，讓師生覺得學習英文是萬分的辛苦。

　　《All in Reading 全方位英文閱讀》這本英文讀本是在考慮上述諸問題的各層面，以及要幫助師生在課堂內能夠培養聽、說、讀、寫四種技能的需求下而編撰的。這本英文讀本的特色就是它照顧了聽、說、讀、寫四種能力的均衡發展；學生既不必為聽力練習多帶一本課本，也不必為英文寫作多帶一本課本，因為本讀本就含有這一類的學習材料。這也就是本書取名「全方位英文閱讀」的原因。

　　筆者編撰此書時，時時刻刻想到老師要如何教，學生要如何學的問題，所以本英文讀本是以課堂教學為導向、以輕鬆有趣為方針、以生活化為原則，相信定能為學習者帶來事半功倍的效益。其中若有疏漏之處，祈請方家不吝指教。

余光雄謹識

|CONTENTS|

Body Decoration

Warm-up

Some people have certain types of decoration on their bodies. Look at the pictures below and answer the following questions.

1. What are these types of body art called?
2. Think of five words to describe how you feel when you see the pictures.

Reading task

Body Decoration

In many cultures, people decorate their bodies with pictures and designs. Sometimes, the human body is painted or colored with dye, which can be washed off later. Other forms of body decoration, such as tattoos, are permanent and stay with the wearer for life. Very often, people decorate their bodies for a particular purpose, which is reflected in the types of patterns that they use.

henna painting

a native of North America

The native people of North America made general use of body painting. When warriors prepared for battle, they would paint themselves with bold designs. These designs were concentrated on their faces, which were decorated with red stripes, black masks or white circles around the eyes. They made the warrior look fierce and aggressive. Other peoples also used warpaint. When the Romans invaded Britain, they found that the ancient

Britons painted themselves with blue paint called "woad" before going into battle.

Body decoration can also be used for occasions other than battles. The Aboriginals of Australia often decorate their bodies with bold white markings for a corroboree. A corroboree is a special meeting at which men dance and sing.

The Maoris of New Zealand decorated their bodies with tattooing. This permanent form of

a Maoris of New Zealand

body decoration indicated the social status of an individual. The more important a person was, the more tattoos he had. Some chiefs and kings had their faces covered entirely by tattoos.

Vocabulary Note

1. decoration *n.* 裝飾
   decorate *v.* 裝飾
2. design *n.* 圖像
3. dye *n.* 染料
4. tattoo *n.* 刺青
5. permanent *adj.* 永久的
6. reflect *v.* 反映
7. warrior *n.* 戰士
8. concentrate *v.* 聚集；集中

9. stripe *n.* 條紋
10. fierce *adj.* 勇猛的
11. aggressive *adj.* 具攻擊性的
12. occasion *n.* 場合
13. Aboriginal *n.* 澳洲原住民
14. status *n.* 地位
15. individual *n.* 個人
16. chief *n.* 酋長

Reading Comprehension Check

According to the text you read, answer the following questions.

( ) 1. What is the main theme of this article?

    (A) People like to decorate their bodies.

    (B) The Aboriginals of Australia like to have body decoration.

    (C) Body decoration is a special kind of art.

    (D) Body decoration is very cultural.

( ) 2. How many kinds of designs were used by the native people of North America on their faces when they were preparing for battle?

    (A) One.   (B) Two.   (C) Three.   (D) More than three.

( ) 3. Which of the following statements is true about tattoos?

    (A) The lower the culture is, the more popular tattoos are.

    (B) Civilized people don't like to have tattoos.

    (C) The North American natives gave up having their tattoos.

    (D) Among the Maoris, tattoos were symbols of social status.

( ) 4. What did the ancient Britons paint their bodies with?

    (A) A kind of blue paint called "woad."

    (B) Any paint, as long as it's blue.

    (C) Green oil paints.

    (D) Watercolors.

( ) 5. Which of the following statements is NOT true?

    (A) In many cultures people don't like to decorate their bodies with designs.

    (B) Tattoos are a permanent form of body decoration.

    (C) The ancient warriors of the North American natives painted their faces to look fierce.

    (D) Chiefs or kings of the Maoris had tattoos on their faces to show social status.

( ) 6. In which culture did people use body decoration as an indication of the social status?

    (A) The Maoris of New Zealand.

    (B) The Aboriginals of Australia.

    (C) The native people of North America.

    (D) The author didn't give examples.

( ) 7. What kind of problems do tattoo wearers have?

    (A) They don't have social status.

    (B) They don't know what kind of patterns to wear.

    (C) They can't wash the tattoos off when they do not want them.

    (D) They have to find doctors to do tattooing for them.

( ) 8. What's the writer's attitude toward body decoration?

    (A) The writer strongly recommends that young people should do it.

    (B) The writer is strongly against body decoration.

    (C) The writer doesn't show his/her preference.

    (D) The writer encourages people to experience this type of body art.

■ Expanding Vocabulary

Part A

Choose the correct answer to complete each sentence. Make changes if necessary.

> woad   corroboree   marking   invade

1. Tattoos are ＿＿＿＿ on the body that can not be easily removed.

2. A ＿＿＿＿ is a special meeting where the Aboriginals of Australia dance and sing to celebrate their culture.

3. The ＿＿＿＿ plant, growing mainly in Europe, is the source of a blue dye.

4. The army ＿＿＿＿ a small village at night and destroyed everything.

a corroboree

5

Part B

Match the words in the left column with the expressions that have similar meaning in the right column.

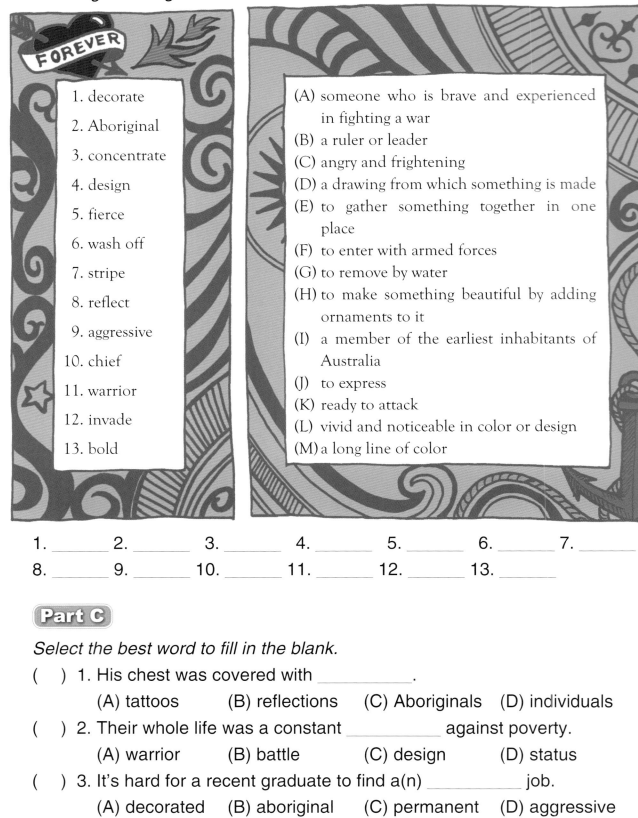

1. decorate	(A) someone who is brave and experienced in fighting a war
2. Aboriginal	(B) a ruler or leader
3. concentrate	(C) angry and frightening
4. design	(D) a drawing from which something is made
5. fierce	(E) to gather something together in one place
6. wash off	(F) to enter with armed forces
7. stripe	(G) to remove by water
8. reflect	(H) to make something beautiful by adding ornaments to it
9. aggressive	(I) a member of the earliest inhabitants of Australia
10. chief	(J) to express
11. warrior	(K) ready to attack
12. invade	(L) vivid and noticeable in color or design
13. bold	(M) a long line of color

1. _____ 2. _____ 3. _____ 4. _____ 5. _____ 6. _____ 7. _____

8. _____ 9. _____ 10. _____ 11. _____ 12. _____ 13. _____

Part C

Select the best word to fill in the blank.

(　) 1. His chest was covered with _____.

    (A) tattoos　　　(B) reflections　　(C) Aboriginals　　(D) individuals

(　) 2. Their whole life was a constant _____ against poverty.

    (A) warrior　　　(B) battle　　　　(C) design　　　　(D) status

(　) 3. It's hard for a recent graduate to find a(n) _____ job.

    (A) decorated　　(B) aboriginal　　(C) permanent　　(D) aggressive

(　　) 4. His writing _____ his concern about the poor in the society.
   (A) decorates (B) reflects (C) masks   (D) invades

(　　) 5. A(n) _____ nation always tries to invade other nations.
   (A) social (B) particular (C) aggressive (D) permanent

(　　) 6. Ms. Wang went to the hair salon to get a hair _____ .
   (A) stripe (B) chief (C) decoration (D) design

(　　) 7. Some people believe that the aliens have been trying to _____ the earth.
   (A) reflect (B) circle (C) cover   (D) invade

(　　) 8. Each _____ is responsible for his/her own life goals.
   (A) design (B) aggression (C) circle   (D) individual

(　　) 9. On some special _____ , a specific dress code must be followed.
   (A) tattoos (B) occasions (C) patterns (D) designs

(　　)10. Tigers and lions are _____ animals.
   (A) aboriginal (B) permanent (C) fierce   (D) individual

Part D

Fill in one proper preposition in the blank.

1. The house was decorated _____ seasonable flowers.
2. We dyed the clothes _____ blue dye.
3. The marks on your arms can be washed _____ .
4. The tattoo _____ the man's body looks so scary.
5. She is looking _____ permanent employment.
6. The tattoo will stay _____ you forever.
7. The army concentrated the force _____ the border and planned to attack the enemy at night.
8. The North American natives often paint their face _____ red stripes.
9. He draws a circle _____ a pencil.
10. John's wife is so aggressive that he is afraid _____ her.
11. This is not an occasion _____ laughter.
12. There are some markings _____ the wall.

S peaking task

■ Conversation Practice

The following conversation talks about body decoration. Practice in pairs.

How much do you know about body decoration?

Tattoos are a permanent form of body decoration. They stay with the wearer forever.

Not much. As far as I know, tattooing is one type.

Do you know how people do tattooing?

People decorate the body with a special kind of dye. At the beginning, the person should choose his or her own design and pattern. After that, the design is colored with various kinds of colors.

I heard that ancient people in some cultures painted their bodies. Did they do body painting for fun?

No. For example, warriors decorated their bodies for a particular purpose. They wanted to look fierce and aggressive.

They painted their faces with scary colors and designs.

How could they look fierce and aggressive?

In addition to battles, are there any other occasions on which body decoration is encouraged?

Yes. The Aboriginals of Australia decorate their bodies with bold white markings for a corroboree, which is a special meeting for men's dancing and singing.

How about in other cultures or countries?

Another example is in New Zealand. The Maoris of New Zealand used different kinds of tattoos to indicate their social status.

Thank you so much for telling me something about body decoration.

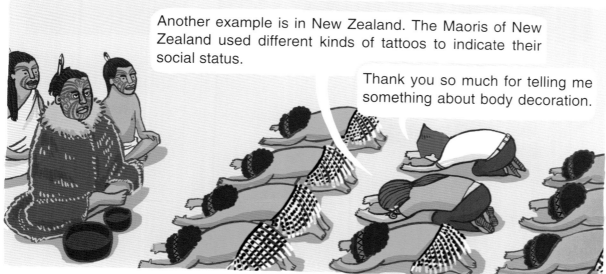

1. as far as one knows　就某人所知
2. at the beginning　一開始
3. in addition to　除了…之外（還…）

▉ Group Discussion ▉

Discuss the following questions with your group members, and then report your answers to the class.

1. What is your group's opinion about having tattoos? Talk about both positive and negative sides of tattooing.
2. Would you like to have some tattoos on your body? Why or why not?
3. Some people use tattoos to express themselves. There is usually a story behind each tattoo. Look at the pictures below. Discuss the possible significance of each tattoo for the wearer.

⌂ Listening task

 Part A

If the sentence you hear on the CD means the same as the sentence you read below, put "S" in the blank; if not, put "D" in the blank.

_____ 1. In many cultures, people decorate their bodies with pictures and designs.

_____ 2. Sometimes, the human body is painted or colored with dye, which can be washed off later.

_____ 3. Tattoos are a permanent form of body decoration and can not be washed off.

_____ 4. The Maoris of New Zealand decorated their bodies to indicate the social status of an individual.

_____ 5. When the warriors of North America prepared for battle, they painted their faces with bold designs.

 **Part B**

If the two sentences on the CD you hear mean the same, put "S" in the blank; if not, put "D" in the blank.

1. _____ 2. _____ 3. _____ 4. _____ 5. _____

 **Part C**

Listen to the conversation on the CD carefully. Check (✓) the true statement about the conversation.

_____ 1. The woman doesn't like her friends to have tattoos on their bodies.

_____ 2. Tattoo stickers can be washed off, while real tattoos are permanent.

_____ 3. Many young people think having tattoos is a kind of fashion.

_____ 4. Young people think that tattoos on their bodies can help them look cool.

_____ 5. The man doesn't think that tattoo stickers can attract young people.

_____ 6. The woman suggests that young people should find out their parents' attitude toward having tattoos on their bodies.

Writing task

■ **Grammar Focus**

Part A

Circle the correct verb form for each sentence.

1. For face painting, the face is coloring/colored with dye and can be removed later.

2. Tattoos can't be washed/washing off later.

3. When warriors prepared for war, they would decorate/decorated their faces with different types of patterns.

4. Body painting can be used/using for occasions other than battles.

5. We may see ourselves reflect/reflected in the clear water.

Part B

Select a proper preposition for each blank.

( ) 1. _____ many cultures, people decorate their bodies with pictures and designs.

(A) With   (B) In   (C) At   (D) From

( ) 2. When warriors prepared _____ battle, they would paint themselves with bold designs.

(A) for   (B) under   (C) of   (D) in

( ) 3. The native people concentrated designs _____ their faces, which were decorated with red stripes, black masks or white circles around the eyes.

(A) at   (B) on   (C) in   (D) with

( ) 4. The Maoris of New Zealand decorated their bodies _____ tattooing.

(A) in   (B) of   (C) with   (D) on

( ) 5. A corroboree is a special meeting _____ which men dance and sing.

(A) for   (B) at   (C) on   (D) from

■ Guided Translation

Translate the Chinese text into English.

人體裝飾，像是刺青，可以是永久性的，也可以用染料上色，並在稍後洗掉。對某些文化裡的原住民來說，刺青象徵著個人的社會地位。現代年輕人喜歡刺青，因為他們認為刺青可以幫助吸引人們的注意，而且看起來很酷。使用刺青貼紙已經成為一種時尚。

Body decoration _____ tattoos can be permanent, and it also can be done _____ _____ which can be _____ _____ later. To the _____ in some cultures, tattoos indicate the _____ _____ of an individual. Modern young people like to have tattoos because they think tattoos can help _____ people's _____ and look _____ . Using tattoo stickers _____ _____ a fashion.

Sentence Patterns

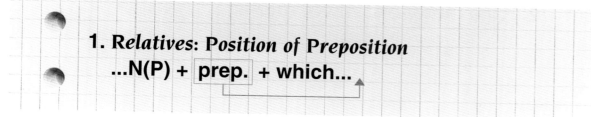

1. Relatives: Position of Preposition

...N(P) + prep. + which...

Example:

a. *Young people like to go to the party.*

b. *At the party they can sing and dance.*

→*Young people like to go to the party **at which** they can sing and dance.*

or *Young people like to go to the party **which** they can sing and dance **at**.*

Exercises:

Combine the two sentences by following the pattern above.

1. { A corroboree is a special party.
{ At the party men and women can dance and sing.

A corroboree is

2. { The bird perches on the nest.
{ In the nest it hatches.

The bird perches

3. { The witch hid in the house.
{ In the house she prepared many sweets for children.

The witch hid

4. { You need to look for the bag.
{ In the bag you will see your birthday present.

5. { She bought the newest edition of this dictionary.
{ For this dictionary she paid about eight hundred dollars.

2. ...the more/-er..., the more/-er....

Examples:

1. In some cultures, **the more important** a person is, **the more** tattoos he has.
2. **The more** exercises you do, **the healthier** you are.

Exercise:

Follow the pattern above to translate each Chinese sentence into English.

1. 天氣越冷，我們穿越多衣服。

   The _____, the _____.

2. 車子越大耗油越多。

   The _____, the _____.

3. 你住的越偏遠，要到市中心就越不方便。

   The _____, the _____.

4. 人越有錢煩惱越多。

   The _____, the _____.

2 Good Luck, Bad Luck

Warm-up

Here are some beliefs about money. Look at the pictures below and check (✓) the correct answer.

1. If you hang up your socks by the toes, _____.

   ☐ you will have more money in two weeks
   ☐ someone will borrow money from you
   ☐ money will slip through your fingers
   ☐ someone will lend you money

2. If you find a coin with tails facing upward, _____.

   ☐ good things will happen to you
   ☐ you will see ghosts
   ☐ you will get the equivalent of the coin
   ☐ you will be unlucky

3. If the palm of your right hand is itchy, _____.

   ☐ you will receive fake coins
   ☐ you will gain money
   ☐ you will lose money
   ☐ you will not be able to save money

Reading task

Good Luck, Bad Luck

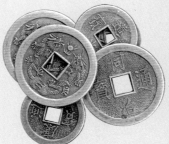

Will you have good luck if you carry a silver coin? Many people believe that carrying a certain coin can bring good luck. Sometimes women wear a coin on a bracelet for luck.

A coin with a hole in it is supposed to be especially lucky in some countries. This idea began long ago, before coins were even used. People believed that a shell or a stone with a hole in it could keep away evil spirits. Coins with a hole would do the same.

There are many other beliefs about how money can bring good luck. Here are a few examples:

· If you find a coin, you will find even more coins.
· A jar of pennies in the kitchen will bring good luck.
· A coin in the bride's shoe at a wedding will lead to a happy marriage.
· If you give a wallet or a purse as a present, put a coin inside. Then the new owner will never be without money.

There are also stories about how money may bring bad luck. One story says that it is unlucky to dream about money. Another story warns about what may happen when you carry coins in a pocket. Shaking the coins and making jangling noises will bring bad luck in love.

Vocabulary Note

1. bracelet *n.* 手鐲
2. suppose *v.* 認為
3. shell *n.* 貝殼
4. keep away 使遠離
5. evil *adj.* 邪惡的
6. spirit *n.* 鬼怪；幽靈
7. belief *n.* 信念，看法

8. jar *n.* 一罐(瓶)的量
9. penny *n.* (美國的)一分銅幣
10. marriage *n.* 婚姻
11. wallet *n.* 皮夾
12. purse *n.* (女用)錢包
13. jangling *adj.* 發出叮噹聲的

■ Reading Comprehension Check ▬▬▬▬

According to the text you read, if the following statement is true, put "T" in the blank; if not, put "F" in the blank.

_____ 1. Carrying a coin may bring people good luck and money.

_____ 2. In some countries, people believe that coins are tokens of good luck.

_____ 3. It is believed that you will not run out of money if you receive, as a present, a wallet with a coin in it.

_____ 4. If you dream of coins, the coins will bring you more money.

_____ 5. Carrying coins in your pocket may bring you good luck.

_____ 6. It is believed that young couple in love should shake the coins and make jangling noises for good luck.

_____ 7. This text mainly deals with superstitions in different cultures.

_____ 8. The author of this text did not show his attitude toward superstition.

■ Expanding Vocabulary ▬▬▬▬▬▬

Part A

Match the words in the left column with the expressions that have similar meanings in the right column.

_____ 1. penny

_____ 2. wedding

_____ 3. evil

_____ 4. belief

_____ 5. wallet

_____ 6. purse

_____ 7. jangling

_____ 8. jar

(A) making a noise of metal hitting metal

(B) a ceremony for getting married

(C) a flat case that holds paper money, coins, cards, etc.

(D) a container used for storing things

(E) a small bag for women to carry money

(F) related to the Devil and other powers that harm people

(G) a coin worth one cent in the U.S.

(H) a strong feeling that something is true or real

Part B

Select the best word to fill in the blank in each sentence.

( ) 1. The fact that many people in the world have seen ghosts shakes my _____ in the non-existence of ghosts.

    (A) belief   (B) legend   (C) wedding   (D) wallet

( ) 2. Do you think Chinese feng shui (風水) is a kind of _____?

    (A) luck   (B) superstition   (C) legend   (D) spirit

( ) 3. It is a superstition that coins can _____ evil spirits and bring good luck.

    (A) keep away   (B) take care of (C) deal with   (D) carry away

( ) 4. The child was given a watch as a _____.

    (A) belief   (B) wedding   (C) present   (D) president

( ) 5. When you meet people for the first time, _____ hands with them firmly.

    (A) rake   (B) bake   (C) brake   (D) shake

( ) 6. People get divorced because they have a broken _____.

    (A) shortage   (B) wallet   (C) marriage   (D) carriage

( ) 7. Red is often used to _____ people about possible danger.

    (A) care   (B) dream   (C) warn   (D) laugh

( ) 8. Receiving a wallet with a coin in it as a present is a sign _____ good luck.

    (A) for   (B) of   (C) with   (D) from

( ) 9. The item that a woman wears around her wrist is called a _____.

    (A) necklace   (B) collar   (C) ring   (D) bracelet

( )10. Scientists still have no evidence to _____ the existence of evil spirits.

    (A) suppose   (B) wear   (C) prove   (D) protect

Part C

Select the best answer to fill in the blank.

Superstitions are often related ___1___ culture and religion. In some cultures, a stone or a shell with a hole in it is said to protect people

_____2_____ evil spirits. Similarly, people think a coin with a hole in it may be accompanied _____3_____ good luck. _____4_____ addition, there are other superstitions about coins bringing good luck. For instance, _____5_____ that if you find a coin, it will bring you many more coins; a coin in the bride's shoe at the wedding is believed to lead _____6_____ a happy marriage. What's more, if you want to give someone a wallet or purse as a present, remember to put a coin inside it. Superstition says that there will always be money inside it, _____7_____, the new owner will never lack money. _____8_____, there are also numerous stories about how money brings bad luck. It is a bad thing to dream _____9_____ money because it will bring bad luck. Other stories say that people _____10_____ better not shake coins and make a jangling sound, because this can mean bad luck too.

(   ) 1. (A) to   (B) with   (C) of   (D) for

(   ) 2. (A) for   (B) to   (C) as   (D) from

(   ) 3. (A) to   (B) as   (C) by   (D) for

(   ) 4. (A) To   (B) With   (C) As   (D) In

(   ) 5. (A) it tells   (B) it is said   (C) people tell   (D) men say

(   ) 6. (A) to   (B) for   (C) forth   (D) up

(   ) 7. (A) furthermore   (B) it is told

            (C) on the contrary   (D) that is to say

(   ) 8. (A) In some way   (B) In another words

            (C) Certainly   (D) On the other hand

(   ) 9. (A) to   (B) of   (C) in   (D) at

(   )10. (A) have   (B) had   (C) would   (D) will

fortune cookies

a four-leaf clover

rabbits' feet

Speaking task

Group Discussion

Form groups of four and discuss the following questions. Report your answers to the class.

1. Give examples of superstitions in your culture and explain their origins, if you know them.

2. How do you feel about believing in superstition? Is it good or bad for people? Why?

3. Many Chinese believe in feng shui. Can you think of some examples? What do you think about them?

4. In many cultures, a black cat is considered unlucky, but in others, it is considered lucky to see a black cat. In your opinion, what's the reason behind these two different beliefs?

5. Look at the pictures below. Try to describe each picture and guess what kind of superstition it talks about.

Role Play

Find a partner to act out the following conversation.

A: Why do you wear bracelets?

B: To protect myself from evil spirits.

A: To protect yourself from evil spirits? I don't understand that.

B: Haven't you heard that a bracelet can protect you from breaking your arms if you fall over?

A: I know that wearing a helmet can protect me from breaking my head. I've never heard about wearing a bracelet can protect me from breaking my arms.

B: Do you think I am superstitious?

A: If you are not superstitious, who is?

 L istening task

Part A

If the sentence you hear on the CD means the same as the one below, put "S" in the blank; if not, put "D" in the blank.

_____ 1. There is a superstition that carrying a coin will bring a person bad luck.

_____ 2. A bracelet with a coin on it can bring people good luck.

_____ 3. Putting a coin in a bride's shoe at the wedding ceremony is believed to lead to a happy marriage.

_____ 4. It is said that people had better not carry coins when they are in the market.

_____ 5. It is bad to believe that dreaming of money will bring a person bad luck.

Part B

You will hear five statements on the CD. Each statement is followed by a question. According to what you hear, select the best answers to the questions.

(   ) 1. (A) Rings and necklaces.   (B) Strings and necklaces.

      (C) Pins and bracelets.   (D) Rings and bracelets.

(   ) 2. (A) Superstition has a long history, even longer than the history of culture.

      (B) Superstition has long existed, and its history is as long as that of coins.

      (C) The history of superstition is longer than that of coins.

      (D) The history of superstition is not longer than that of coins.

(   ) 3. (A) It will bring bad luck.   (B) It will scare away evil spirits.

      (C) It will mean a happy marriage.(D) It will lead to a tragic ending.

(   ) 4. (A) We need to find out more information about the history of coins.

      (B) More superstitions about coins can't be found.

      (C) There are more superstitions about coins to be discovered.

      (D) The world has a trend of discovering all the superstitions about coins.

(   ) 5. (A) Put an empty jar in the kitchen.

      (B) Put some money on the kitchen floor.

      (C) Put a jar of pennies in the kitchen.

      (D) Put some pennies in the pocket of the jacket.

Writing task

■ Writing Practice

Combine each pair of sentences into one.

1. ⎰ It is a superstition.

   ⎱ Carrying a coin will bring people good luck.

→ _____

2. { Many women wear bracelets.
    { The bracelets are decorated with coins.

    →

3. { The story is related to the belief.
    { The belief is that carrying coins will bring good luck.

    →

4. { You will have good luck.
    { You put a jar of pennies in the kitchen.

    →

■ Grammar Focus

There are several grammatical errors in each sentence below. Identify them and rewrite each sentence in the blanks.

1. Have you ever think that you've been lucky because of you own a silver coin?

2. There are a superstition that carry a coin will bring people good luck.

3. However, many woman wear bracelets is a token of good luck.

4. This superstition is relating to the belief which things such as stone or shells would protect them from evil souls and spirits.

5. Superstition got started long before, before coins were using .

▋Guided Writing

Look at the following pictures about Taiwanese superstitions and write down what they mean. Follow the example.

Example:

The number "four" sounds like the word "death" in Chinese and was considered unlucky. Therefore, some places like hotels and hospitals don't have a fourth floor and the numbers in an elevator jump from three to five.

_____

_____

_____

_____

_____

_____

_____

_____

_____

_____

_____

_____

_____

_____

_____

3 Language in Clothes

Warm-up

People wear different colors and clothes for different occasions. Look at the clothing items below and answer the following questions.

sleeveless blouse   mini-skirt   jacket   jean skirt   straight skirt

dress   pants   shirt   T-shirt   high-heeled shoes

Jenny

flats   sandals   briefcase   handbag   weave bag

1. There are four occasions for Jenny to attend. Choose appropriate clothing for each occasion for her from these items.
   (A) A birthday party.   (B) A funeral.
   (C) A music concert.   (D) A business meeting.

2. Based on what you chose for Jenny for each occasion, explain your choice of the items.

Reading task

Language in Clothes

Wearing clothes not only covers and protects our bodies but has other meanings. Sometimes people wear particular styles to give out a message. Sometimes they wear certain clothes to suit the occasion.

A T-shirt with a message is a very obvious form of communication in clothing. The T-shirt may carry the name of a pop group, club or organization. This clothing shows the musical taste of the wearer, or tells everyone that he or she supports a particular club. Some people wear a T-shirt with the name of a product as a form of advertising.

Sometimes people wear specific clothes for special occasions. When a western woman gets married, she may wear an expensive wedding dress, which is much longer and more elaborate than her normal choice of dress. A western man getting married might wear a top hat and tails, neither of which he would wear in ordinary life. Different cultures and religions have different traditions about wedding clothes. At Christian weddings, it is usual for the bride to wear white. Hindus and Sikhs often wear very brightly colored clothes. A Chinese bride may wear an outfit decorated with embroidered dragons and phoenixes, which are signs of good luck.

All these special clothes show that the couple considers marriage to be a joyful and unique event. When attending funerals, by contrast, people in many different cultures normally wear dark clothes, sometimes with a black tie or an armband. This is because black is a sign of a sorrowful mood.

a couple in a Hindu wedding

Vocabulary Note

1. particular *adj.* 特定的；特殊的
2. obvious *adj.* 明顯的
3. organization *n.* 組織；機構
4. product *n.* 產品
5. specific *adj.* 特定的；特殊的
6. occasion *n.* 場合
7. elaborate *adj.* 精緻的
8. tail *n.* (常做複數) 燕尾服
9. outfit *n.* (特殊場合的) 全套服裝
10. embroidered *adj.* 刺繡的
11. funeral *n.* 喪禮
12. armband *n.* 臂環
13. sorrowful *adj.* 哀傷的

■Reading Comprehension Check ■

Part A

Match the following items in the box with those in the bottom box. The first one has been done for you.

1. People wear a T-shirt with the name of an organization...
2. A T-shirt that carries the name of a product...
3. At Christian weddings, ...
4. At Hindu and Sikh weddings, ...
5. People wear dark clothes...

(A) ...to funerals to show their sorrowful moods.
(B) ...a bride often wears a longer and more elaborate dress than usual.
(C) ...is a form of advertising.
(D) ...to show their support.
(E) ...brides wear something bright and colorful.

1. _D_   2. _____   3. _____   4. _____   5. _____

Part B

According to the text you read, answer the following questions.

( ) 1. What do dragons and phoenixes on a Chinese outfit signify?

(A) A blessing from God.
(B) Good luck for the bride.
(C) Wealth and fame of the bride's family.
(D) The excellent handiwork of the dress maker.

( ) 2. What is the main idea of the third paragraph of the text you read?
   (A) People wear specific clothes for special occasions.
   (B) Brides wear white dresses for their weddings.
   (C) Hindus like to wear brightly colored clothes.
   (D) Different kinds of clothes indicate different kinds of luck.

( ) 3. Read the paragraph in the box below. Then choose one statement from (A) to (D) that best describes the textual relationship between the sentences in the paragraph.

A T-shirt with a message is a very obvious form of communication in clothing. The T-shirt may carry the name of a pop group, club or organization. This clothing shows the musical taste of the wearer, or tells everyone that he or she supports a particular club. Some people wear a T-shirt with the name of a product as a form of advertising.

(A) The first sentence is a topic sentence, and the rest are supporting sentences.
(B) The last sentence is a topic sentence, and the rest give supporting ideas.
(C) The second sentence illustrates the first, and the last supports the third.
(D) All these four sentences can be rearranged in any order we like.

■ Expanding Vocabulary

Part A

( ) 1. When attending a _____, people normally wear dark clothes.
   (A) wedding   (B) funeral   (C) meeting   (D) lecture
( ) 2. Following _____ can be quite expensive.
   (A) crowds   (B) instincts   (C) footsteps   (D) fashions

(　　) 3. She sees off a good friend, her eyes being full of _____ tears.

(A) sorrowful　　(B) moody　　　　(C) funeral　　　(D) elaborate

(　　) 4. He gave a(n) _____ answer to the question.

(A) elaborate　　(B) tailed　　　　(C) occasional　　(D) colored

(　　) 5. He wore a cap with a(n) _____ star mark.

(A) suitable　　(B) bride　　　　(C) decoration　　(D) embroidered

(　　) 6. _____ is what you wear to cover and decorate your body.

(A) Clothing　　(B) Wearing　　　(C) Fashion　　　(D) Funeral

(　　) 7. ETS stands for Educational Testing Service, which is a(n) _____ that takes charge of TOEFL tests.

(A) reference　　(B) organization　(C) occasion　　(D) permanence

(　　) 8. It is _____ that English has become an international language.

(A) fashionable　(B) occasional　　(C) obvious　　　(D) organizational

(　　) 9. Taiwan makes money by exporting industrial _____.

(A) clothing　　(B) products　　　(C) suits　　　　(D) tattoos

(　　)10. The Taiwanese _____ their house with couplets written on red papers during Chinese New Year.

(A) decorate　　(B) design　　　　(C) elaborate　　(D) participate

Part B

Some adjectives can be formed from a noun by adding a suffix "-al" or "-able" to the end of the word. Try to form an adjective for each of the following.

Noun	Adjective
1. organization	organizational
2. fashion	
3. music	
4. occasion	
5. norm	
6. culture	

Part C

介系詞片語(Prepositional Phrase)可作形容詞，用來修飾名詞，使該名詞的訊息更完整。請依照提示的字，用適當的介系詞合併下列名詞。

1. body painting (many cultures)   body painting in many cultures
2. clothes (particular)
3. a T-shirt (message)
4. musical taste (wearer)
5. T-shirt (the name/a product)
6. an outfit (embroidered/dragons/phoenixes)

Speaking task

▌Group Discussion

Answer each of the following questions. Discuss your answers with your group members.

1. What would you like to wear if you are getting married?

2. What do the embroidered dragons and phoenixes on the outfit of a Chinese bride represent?

3. It seems that women follow clothes fashions more faithfully than men. Give your opinion about this phenomenon.

4. What kind of clothes are you wearing today? Show the class your outfit and explain why you chose to wear those clothes today.

■Role Play

Find a partner to act out the following conversation.

A: Your friend wears a new dress today and you praise her dress. Ask about the style of the dress and why she decided to wear it today.

B: You appreciate your friend's compliment and describe the dress you are wearing.

(Change roles and try the role play again.)

  **istening task**

Part A

If the two sentences on the CD you hear mean the same, put "S" in the blank; if not, put "D" in the blank.

1. _____   2. _____   3. _____   4. _____   5. _____

Listen to the eight sentences on the CD. Eunice (E) and Buck (B) are making a statement about each sentence. Choose whose statement is correct.

1. ☐ E: A T-shirt with a message has nothing to do with communication.
   ☐ B: Sometimes people express themselves by wearing particular types of clothes.
2. ☐ E: A wedding dress is the same kind of clothing as we wear every day.
   ☐ B: A wedding dress is more important than daily clothes.
3. ☐ E: People usually wear black clothes to attend a funeral.
   ☐ B: Green is a color that signifies a sorrowful mood.
4. ☐ E: We can advertise a product by wearing a T-shirt with the product's name on it.
   ☐ B: We can advertise a product by selling T-shirts on the streets.
5. ☐ E: Traditions about wedding clothes vary from culture to culture.
   ☐ B: Most cultures have the same tradition about wedding clothes.
6. ☐ E: People may support an organization by making donations.
   ☐ B: People wear a T-shirt with the name of an organization to show their support.
7. ☐ E: We can know someone's taste by what he/she wears.
   ☐ B: People don't usually think about what to wear.
8. ☐ E: A Chinese bride may wear a white dress on her wedding day.
   ☐ B: A Chinese woman may wear an outfit with embroidered dragons and phoenixes on her wedding day.

Writing task

Grammar Focus

There are a few grammatical errors in the following passage. Underline the errors, and write the correct answers in the box given below the passage.

All these special clothes shows that the couple consider marriage is a joy event. Therefore, when a woman gets married, she may wear a wedding dress, that is much longer and elaborator than her normal clothes. For example, a Chinese bride may wear an outfit which decorated with embroidered dragons and phoenixes.

On contrast, When attend funerals, people in many different culture normal wear dark clothes, sometime with a black tie or armband. Black is a sign of a sorrow mood.

Error	Correction

Sentence Completion

Part A

Based on the content of the text you have read, complete each of the following sentences in your own words.

1. A Chinese bride may wear   .
2. A T-shirt with a name of a pop group   .
3. Wearing clothes can   .
4. People wear particular styles in order to   .
5. Chinese people consider a wedding   .

Part B

Fill in one proper word to make the passage coherent.

People often wear clothes ¹_____ have particular styles and fashions in order to give out a message ²_____ tells others what kind of person the wearer is.

For example, a T-shirt ³_____ has a message is a very obvious form of communication in clothing. A T-shirt ⁴_____ carries the name of a club or organization is communicating a message through ⁵_____ we can learn something about the wearer. ⁶_____, this type of clothing shows the wearer's tastes, or tells everyone ⁷_____ he or she supports a particular club. ⁸_____, wearing clothes is not simply about putting on garments. We are what we wear.

▪ Paragraph Writing

In the following given situation, write a paragraph of 80 words in length to give your opinions on wearing clothes.

Do you think clothes can really convey what the wearer thinks, or do you think clothes are merely things that cover your body and keep you warm?

UNIT 4

Animal Communication

Warm-up

Look at the pictures below and answer the following questions.

1. What are these animals doing? What do they want to express?
2. Do you know any ways animals exchange information with others?

Reading task

Animal Communication

Although body language is an important part of animal mating rituals, it is a vital means of communication in many other situations too. Many animals have greeting rituals. When different members of the same species meet in the wild, they may be uncertain whether they are facing an enemy or a friend. So they go through careful greeting rituals to make sure that the other animal does not intend to attack.

Other animals make special signals to warn the members of their species that there is danger nearby. One kind of deer in

a white-tailed deer

a flying honeybee

North America has a white tail. When it is frightened, it runs away with its white tail held upright in the air. The other deer see this warning sign and know to run away too.

Honeybees also use body signals to pass on information. They spend the summer collecting pollen and nectar from flowers to make honey.

a frightened chimpanzee

During the winter, this honey will provide them with food. If a bee finds a large group of flowers, it returns to the hive. There it "dances," flying around in a figure of eight, waggling and shaking its body as it does so. When the other bees see these movements, they learn where the flowers are and fly out to harvest the pollen.

Like humans, animals also express their moods and feelings through facial expressions. Chimpanzees open their mouths wide and show their teeth when they are frightened or excited. They often pout as a sign of greeting. When they want to look threatening, they press their lips together and jut out their jaws.

Vocabulary Note

1. mating n. 交配
2. ritual n. 例行性活動
3. species n. 物種
4. signal n. 信號
5. hive n. 蜂巢
6. waggle v. 搖動、來回擺動
7. expression n. 表情
8. pout v. 噘嘴
9. jut out 伸出、突出

■ Reading Comprehension Check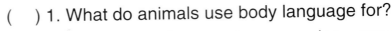

According to the text, select the best answer to the questions.

(　) 1. What do animals use body language for?

(A) For mating and expressing specific information and feelings.

(B) For showing gestures and sounds so as to make friends with other species.

(C) For giving a beautiful appearance to attract animals of other species.

(D) For scaring away the members of their species.

(　) 2. When would a kind of deer in North America raise its white tail?

(A) When it mates.

(B) When it guides the deer behind it.

(C) When it shows off its beautiful tail.

(D) When it warns other deer of the danger nearby.

(　) 3. How do honeybees tell other bees where the food is?

(A) They tell others with buzzing sounds.

(B) They fly around in a figure of eight.

(C) They wave their wings to tell others to follow them.

(D) They tell other bees directly in bees' language.

(　) 4. Which animals use facial expressions like human beings do?

(A) Chimpanzees.　　　　　(B) American deer.

(C) Honeybees.　　　　　　(D) Dogs.

(　) 5. What do chimpanzees do when they want to look threatening?

(A) They roar threateningly.

(B) They wave their strong fists.

(C) They jut out their jaws.

(D) They throw rocks toward enemies.

■ Reading for Details

According to the text you read, select one proper word for each blank.

As well as in mating rituals, body language is a(n) ¹_____ part of animal communication in other situations. Animals, like ²_____, can also use some signals to express specific meanings, such as greetings, warnings, conveyance of information, and feelings. Let's ³_____ some animal behavior for example. Some animals would make a ⁴_____ greeting when they are uncertain ⁵_____ members of the same species are friends or enemies. In North America, one kind of deer would raise its white tail ⁶_____ the air to warn other deer to run ⁷_____ when it ⁸_____ danger nearby. When honeybees find a group of flowers, they would go back to their ⁹_____ and "dance" in a figure of eight, ¹⁰_____ their bodies, to tell other bees where the pollen and nectar are.

( ) 1. (A) special   (B) important   (C) small   (D) useful
( ) 2. (A) plants   (B) computers
       (C) human beings   (D) music
( ) 3. (A) take   (B) make   (C) use   (D) do
( ) 4. (A) indifferent (B) careful   (C) hostile   (D) enthusiastic
( ) 5. (A) that   (B) which   (C) as   (D) whether
( ) 6. (A) in   (B) on   (C) above   (D) around
( ) 7. (A) across   (B) after   (C) down   (D) away
( ) 8. (A) walks   (B) looks   (C) touches   (D) finds
( ) 9. (A) house   (B) hive   (C) cage   (D) nest
( ) 10. (A) waggle and shake   (B) waggling and shaken
        (C) waggling and shaking   (D) waggled and shaken

■ Expanding Vocabulary

Part A

Learn the definitions of the new words. Match the words on the left with the definitions on the right.

1. upright	(A) to bring things together from different places
2. collect	(B) to move from side to side or up and down
3. nectar	(C) a place where bees live
4. hive	(D) in vertical and straight position
5. waggle	(E) a sweet liquid produced by flowers
6. pout	(F) to push out lips to show anger

1. _____ 2. _____ 3. _____ 4. _____ 5. _____ 6. _____

7. excited	(G) a set of fixed actions performed regularly
8. communication	(H) an action to give information
9. ritual	(I) happy and interested because of things which are going to happen
10. signal	(J) the process of exchanging information or expressing feelings
11. threatening	(K) intending to harm
12. pollen	(L) a fine powder from flowers

7. _____ 8. _____ 9. _____ 10. _____ 11. _____ 12. _____

Part B

Match two words which have opposite meaning to each other.

1. vital	(A) tame
2. wild	(B) unimportant
3. uncertain	(C) defend
4. attack	(D) sure
5. danger	(E) far
6. nearby	(F) safety

1. _____ 2. _____ 3. _____ 4. _____ 5. _____ 6. _____

■ Word in Use

Select the best word to fill in each blank.

(   ) 1. The issues presented at the meeting are of _____ importance.

        (A) vital   (B) ritual   (C) virtual   (D) complicated

(   ) 2. _____ is the major function of language.

        (A) Intervention   (B) Communication

        (C) Complication   (D) Interpretation

(   ) 3. It is a Chinese _____ to worship ancestors on New Year's Day.

        (A) ritual   (B) recital   (C) respect   (D) rural

(   ) 4. Our army _____ the enemy's camp during the night.

        (A) attacked   (B) arrested   (C) dispatched   (D) disclosed

(   ) 5. A red light is usually a _____ used to signify a dangerous situation.

        (A) lamp   (B) significance   (C) signal   (D) lantern

(   ) 6. Please adjust the seat to a(n) _____ position.

        (A) prospective (B) upcoming   (C) applicable   (D) upright

(   ) 7. There is no way of knowing the number of bees in their _____.

        (A) dwelling   (B) residence   (C) home   (D) hive

(   ) 8. The child waited for his mother for so long that he _____ his legs impatiently.

        (A) waved   (B) frightened   (C) waggled   (D) changed

(   ) 9. Bees busily collect _____ from flowers in summer.

        (A) pollution   (B) population   (C) potential   (D) pollen

(   ) 10. Chimpanzees _____ when they greeted each other.

        (A) spout   (B) pout   (C) shout   (D) strain

(   ) 11. The coming storm seems to be _____. The sky has turned dark now.

        (A) treated   (B) threatening   (C) thawed   (D) threading

(   ) 12. The country must have _____ many wars. Buildings in the cities are all damaged.

        (A) gone over   (B) gone through

        (C) passed through   (D) passed over

(　) 13. Chimpanzees open their mouths wide and show their teeth when they are _____.

(A) collected　(B) greeted　(C) patted　(D) frightened

(　) 14. The teacher asked students to _____ the handouts _____ to the next person.

(A) give, out　(B) pass, down　(C) pass, on　(D) divide, up

(　) 15. Animals, like human beings, show their moods and feelings _____ facial expressions.

(A) through　(B) in
(C) with　(D) from

Phrase Drill

Select a proper phrase listed to complete each sentence. Changes of word forms might be necessary.

| go through | run away | pass on | make sure | jut out |

1. He had _____ lots of hardship before he achieved success.
2. We can't _____ that the meeting time is at 3 o'clock.
3. The criminal broke the window and _____.
4. The teacher asked me to _____ the book _____ to the classmate sitting behind me.
5. When a chimp is angry, it _____ its jaw to look fierce.

 Speaking task

■Group Discussion

Discuss the following questions with your group members. Then, report your answers to the class.

1. Except for the examples given in the article, can you think of other examples of how animals communicate with each other?

2. How do human beings greet each other? Do these rituals mean the same as those of other animals?

3. Do you have pets? Have you ever observed the way they communicate with each other? Give some examples according to your experiences.

■Conversation Practice

Find a partner to practice the following conversation.

Worker Bee: I've found lots of pollen over there!

Queen Bee: Where exactly?

Worker Bee: The pollen is on the tall red roses over there.

Queen Bee: How far is it from here? Can you be a little more specific?

Worker Bee: It's not too far from here. Watch me. (The bee starts dancing.)

Queen Bee: Yes, it's not too far from here. In what direction?

Worker Bee: Look at the angles of my dance.

Queen Bee: Got it. Everybody, listen. Let's follow Worker Bee to collect pollen.

istening task

Part A

Listen to the CD. You will hear two descriptions of each following sentence. Choose the correct description which has the same meaning as the sentence.

( ) 1. Animals use body language as a means of communication.

( ) 2. Animals go through specific processes to identify whether they are facing a friend or an enemy.

( ) 3. The reason why animals perform certain rituals is to make sure that the other animal of their own species won't attack them.

( ) 4. Dancing in a figure of eight is the way that honeybees use to show the direction of flowers.

( ) 5. Like human beings, chimpanzees use facial expressions to show their moods and feelings.

( ) 6. While in danger, chimpanzees usually jut out their jaws to look threatening.

Part B

Listen to the sentences on the CD carefully, and fill in the missing words in the blanks.

1. As well as in mating _____ , body language plays an important part in animal communication.

2. When the deer in North America are _____ , they give a sign to other deer with their tails held _____ in the air.

3. Animals make careful _____ when they are _____ whether the same _____ they meet are friends or enemies.

4. Honeybees tell their fellow bees where the _____ and _____ are.

5. Like human beings, _____ make some _____ expressions.

Writing task

Guided Writing

Answer the following questions in your own words.

After reading the text, can you describe how honeybees tell other bees the direction of the food?

Chimpanzees use body language to communicate. Can you think of any examples of how chimpanzees show feelings by facial expressions?

Look! The deer is running with its tail held upright! What is it doing this for?

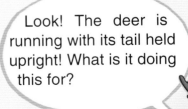

Sentence Completion

1. 動物像人類一樣，也會用臉部表情來溝通。

   Like _____ , animals communicate with _____ .

2. 肢體語言對人類來説是一種非常重要的溝通方式。

   Body language is considered _____ for human beings.

3. 那隻狗非常害怕，因為男孩發出很大的聲音。

   The _____ dog _____

   because the boy made a loud noise.

4. 那隻狗逃走的時候，把牠的長尾巴直挺挺的舉在空中。

   The dog ran away with its long tail _____ .

5. 上課鐘響，老師用手勢暗示學生安靜下來。

   The bell rang and the teacher _____ to keep quiet.

Sentence Patterns

> **1. ...make sure + of + N....**
> **= ...make sure (that)....**

The idiom "make sure" is used to show that you take action purposefully to check that something is true, has been done, or something else happens.

Exercises:

Translate the following Chinese into English with the words given.

1. 你最好確定他明天會到台北。(make sure of)

2. 她確認已經打掃過房間了。(make sure that)

3. 我無法確定每件事都是完美無缺的。(make sure that)

4. 我願意花一生的時間來確保她的幸福。(make sure of)

5. 請務必把這個資訊傳遞給他。(make sure that)

6. 颱風來臨前，務必做好防颱準備。(Make sure that)

 2. S + V, V-ing....

Examples:

1. The girl cried, and she told her mother that she was afraid of dark.

→ The girl cried, telling her mother that she was afraid of dark.

2. John walked into the classroom, and he smiled at everyone.

→ John walked into the classroom, smiling at everyone.

Exercises:

1. The kids jumped up and down on the bed, and they sang the song they learned in the school today.

   →

2. My mom went out to the market, and she left my brother and me home.

   →

3. Mary stayed at the office, and she worked until midnight.

   →

4. The book is very popular, and it has sold five million copies worldwide.

   →

5. Father was cleaning the room, and he swept the floor carefully.

   →

5 Take a Walk

Warm-up

Read the facts about walking below and discuss the following questions with the class.

✓ Every minute of walking can make your life longer by 1.5 to 2 minutes.

✓ You have to walk through a whole football field to burn off ONE plain M & M's chocolate candy.

✓ Walking every day can help you reduce the rate of breast cancer by 20 percent, heart disease by 30 percent, and diabetes by 50 percent.

✓ Walking an extra 20 minutes every day can help you burn off 3 kilograms of body fat per year.

1. Do you think walking is a type of exercise? Why or why not?
2. In your opinion, what's the difference between walking and jogging?

Reading task

Take a Walk

Many people run for sport or exercise. But what if you are not a "born" runner or jogger? You may still want a sport that's inexpensive and easy to do. Why not try walking?

Walking is something that almost any normal, healthy person can do. It requires no special equipment. Walking can give you many of the same benefits as jogging or running; it will just take longer. Jogging and running make your heart and lungs work harder than walking. They also put more stress on your legs and feet than walking does.

The problem with walking as a kind of exercise is that most people don't take it seriously. But there's a big difference between serious walking and the kind of walking that most of us do. Walking, like jogging, should have a steady and continuous motion.

walking as an easy sport

a steady and continuous motion

If you're going to get your exercise by walking, you need to have your own walking program. After all, runners and joggers set goals for themselves. Walkers need goals, too.

Set a definite course to walk. Start by walking about 15 to 30 minutes a day. Build up your time and distance slowly. Try increasing your walking speed little by little.

If jogging or running is your sport, follow the same advice. Start off slowly. Spend most of the first few days just walking. Then start walking and running on the same day. Run or jog a short distance, then walk for a while, then run, then walk. Follow that pattern for 15 to 30 minutes a day. Slowly make each run longer and each walk shorter. Later on, you can increase your distance, speed, and exercise time.

Vocabulary Note

1. require *v.* 需要
2. equipment *n.* 設備
3. benefit *n.* 好處
4. stress *n.* 壓力
5. steady *adj.* 穩定的
6. continuous *adj.* 連續的
7. motion *n.* 動作
8. set *v.* 安排，訂立
9. goal *n.* 目標
10. definite *adj.* 確定的，不會改變的
11. course *n.* 路線

■ Reading Comprehension Check

According to the text you read, if the statement is true, circle "T"; if not, circle "F."

T F 1. Walking requires special equipment.

T F 2. Walking puts more stress on your heart and lungs than jogging.

T F 3. Most people don't take walking seriously as a kind of exercise.

T F 4. Walking has the same benefits as running.

T F 5. We should set a definite course when we walk.

T F 6. Walkers should set goals for themselves.

T F 7. Walkers may start by walking about 15 to 30 minutes a day.

T F 8. Walking put more stress on our feet than jogging does.

■ Expanding Vocabulary

Part A

Select the best word to fill in the blank.

(   ) 1. Something that doesn't cost much is _____.
   (A) indefinite　　(B) uncertain　　(C) inexpensive　(D) unnecessary

(   ) 2. To do a science project normally _____ time and energy.
   (A) requires　　(B) expects　　(C) costs　　(D) increases

(   ) 3. A good university should have excellent professors as well as advanced _____.
   (A) equipment　(B) occasion　　(C) requirement　(D) continuity

(   ) 4. Successful people usually set themselves _____ for their careers.
   (A) motion　　(B) benefit　　(C) stress　　(D) goals

(   ) 5. My friend Kevin often says "I am _____. I'm not joking" when he really means it.
   (A) happy　　(B) laughing　　(C) hard　　(D) serious

Part B

Fill in one proper word in each blank.

1. Walking does not _____ as much stress _____ legs and feet as jogging does.

2. If you want to have good grades, the homework the teacher gives you should be _____ seriously.

3. Most successful businessmen _____ goals _____ themselves at an early age.

4. New students should _____ the advice given by seniors so as to improve their grades.

5. If we want to get some exercise _____ walking, we need to have our own walking programs.

6. As for jogging, you may slowly make each run longer and each walk shorter. _____ _____, you can join a long-distance race.

7. Do your students have problems _____ accurate pronunciation when speaking English?

8. If you are going to _____ jogging _____ your exercise, start slowly and increase your jogging time and distance little by little, or you may get hurt.

9. Why not take a bus to the office? It's _____ because it wouldn't cost a lot of money.

10. If you want to be a successful man, set a goal for yourself. _____ _____, you have to take responsibility for your own life.

peaking task

Group Discussion

Form groups of four and discuss the following questions. Report your answers to the class.

1. For what reasons do people run?
2. What equipment do people need for running or jogging?
3. What are the similarities and differences between running, jogging, and walking?
4. What kind of sports do you like? Why?

Role Play

Work in pairs. Discuss the sport each of you likes the most. Include the following subjects in your discussion.

1. The name of your favorite sport.
2. The reasons why you like the sport.
3. The amount of time you spend on the sport.
4. The similarities and differences between the two sports.

◉ ▮Conversation Practice ▬▬▬▬

Practice the following conversation in pairs.

Kathy: What kind of sports do you like, Helen?

Helen: I like to play tennis. What about you?

Kathy: I like jogging because it is very easy.

Helen: How much time do you spend jogging every week?

Kathy: About one hour. How about you with tennis?

Helen: About two hours. However, sometimes I have difficulty finding a partner.

Kathy: That's why I like jogging. I can jog alone.

Helen: But it's more fun to play with friends.

Kathy: Yes, jogging is sometimes kind of lonely.

Helen: Then why don't you play tennis or other sports with your friends?

Kathy: My friends don't like to exercise.

Helen: You can tell them it's beneficial to exercise regularly.

Kathy: You know, it's very hard to get those couch potatoes off their sofas, but I'll try.

Helen: That would be great! We can play tennis together, and we'll have fun!

Listening task

Part A

Listen to the CD. According to what you hear, select the best answer to each question.

(   ) 1. Which of the following is NOT mentioned by the two speakers?

    (A) Controlling weight is not easy.

    (B) Most people are not born runners.

    (C) Walking is another way of weight control.

    (D) The speakers are concerned with weight control.

(   ) 2. Which of the following is NOT true?

    (A) Walking is an inexpensive sport.

    (B) Walking has the same benefits as jogging.

    (C) Walking is a steady and continuous motion.

    (D) Walking does not need a good plan.

(   ) 3. What problem does the woman have?

    (A) She can't control her weight.

    (B) She needs to put on some weight.

    (C) She needs to go on a special diet.

    (D) She needs exercise such as jogging and running.

(   ) 4. What does the woman mean by "You need to set goals for yourself"?

    (A) You need to decide how much you'd like to spend on buying equipment.

    (B) You need to decide what you want to be in the future.

    (C) You need to decide whether you want to be a professional athlete or not.

    (D) You need to decide how long and where you want to walk.

before

( ) 5. What does the man mean by "I just can't wait"?

(A) He is running out of time.

(B) He has something to do immediately.

(C) He would like to try walking as a kind of exercise.

(D) He can't wait for the woman to work together.

Part B

Listen to the CD and answer the following questions.

( ) 1. In order to make walking a habit, how long do you need to do it continuously?

(A) Three days. (B) Two weeks. (C) Four weeks. (D) Four months.

( ) 2. Which of the following is NOT a benefit of walking mentioned on the CD?

(A) It puts less stress on your legs.

(B) It makes you think clearly.

(C) It helps you lose weight.

(D) It's easy to prepare the equipment.

( ) 3. According to the CD, what is the equipment you need when walking?

(A) A pair of shoes.   (B) Loose clothes.

(C) A pair of sunglasses.   (D) A bottle of water.

after

( ) 4. According to the CD, how long should you walk a day?

(A) You should walk 15 minutes a day and shouldn't expand the time you walk.

(B) The time you spend walking shouldn't be over 15 minutes a day.

(C) Walk 15 minutes a day then gradually increase the time you walk.

(D) Walk 15 minutes a day then decrease your walking time little by little.

■ Sentence Patterns

Use the given structures to translate each of the following into English.

 1. Why not + V...?

Examples:

1. Why not go to the movies with me?

2. Why not take a rest and relax yourself?

Exercises:

Translate the following Chinese sentences into English ones.

1. 為何不清理廚房呢？

2. 為何不喝水來代替汽水呢？

3. 為何不花一百元買這本字典呢？

4. 為何不去慢跑呢？

5. 為何不去海邊度假呢？

6. 為何不買個蛋糕為她慶祝生日呢？

2. ...spend + $\begin{Bmatrix} \text{time} \\ \text{money} \end{Bmatrix}$ **+ (on) + V-ing....**

Examples:

1. *You need to spend 30 minutes (on) walking every morning.*
2. *Is it really worth spending 20,000 NTD (on) buying a name-brand handbag?*

Exercises:

Translate the following Chinese sentences into English ones.

1. 她花了三年寫成這本書。

2. 我們花五千元買這個錶。

3. 媽媽花了一整個早上為我們準備午餐。

4. 爸爸花了五十萬買這台車。

5. 這個導演花了三年的時間製作這部電影。

■ Translation

Complete each of the following sentences.

1. 讓我們為自由與民主而跑。

   Let us _____ .

2. 從事戶外活動的困難之處就是可能會下雨。

   The _____ is that it may rain.

3. 試著漸漸增加你的跑步時間。

Try increasing your running time _____ .

4. 如果你想藉由節食來維持健康，你需要替自己設定目標。

If you want to _____ by _____ , you need to

_____ for yourself.

5. 很多人沒有嚴肅的看待誠實這件事。

Many people do not _____ seriously.

■ Guided Writing

Translate the following Chinese passage into English.

健康專家説人是會動的動物，但是如果坐久了，就會變成植物；躺久了就會變成礦物。所以運動對人是很重要的。走路是一種很容易做的運動。首先，作好計畫，定好目標，持之以恆，慢慢地你就會很健康。

Health experts say that _____ , but if they

_____ , they become plants; if they

_____ , they become minerals. Therefore

exercise is _____ . Walking is a kind of exercise

_____ . First of all, you have to _____

_____ , _____ , and do it persistently.

_____ , you will be healthy.

Accepting Compliments

Warm-up

Here are four pictures of different kinds of compliments in four cultures. Look at the following conversations and choose a correct picture for each of them.

A.

Nepal

B.

The Netherlands

C.

India

D.

Russia

( ) 1. a: Nice pair of gloves!

b: You can have them if you like.

( ) 2. a: You really have a big belly!

b: Oh, thank you. I ate a lot lately.

( ) 3. a: I'm done here. The dinner is delicious.

b: I'm glad you like it.

( ) 4. a: What do you think of my garden?

b: Not bad.

Accepting Compliments

Everyone needs a pat on the back now and then, but compliments are often easier to give than to receive, especially for Americans. Tell an American that he or she plays a great game of tennis, and the compliment will probably be shrugged off with "It must be my lucky day" or "This new racket is wonderful" or "My tennis teacher is fantastic!" Of course, a person might also smile and say "Thank you," but many Americans downplay compliments by giving the credit to someone or something else.

It is interesting to compare how people from different cultures react to compliments. In some countries, if you compliment someone on a possession, he or she will give it to you or tell you that you may use it whenever you like. In some countries, a person will make a derogatory remark about it or accept praise with humility and unworthiness. But in most cultures, compliments are received with gratitude.

A current form of complimenting is referred to as stroking, the praise or positive feedback people give each other especially in the workplace. American companies understand the importance of giving recognition to employees in order to maintain morale and assure workers' performance. Companies often give rewards for outstanding achievements and service.

Vocabulary Note

1. compliment *n.* 恭維，讚許
2. a pat on the back　讚美，鼓勵
3. shrug off　一笑置之；不理會
4. fantastic *adj.* 極好的，了不起的
5. downplay *v.* 將…輕描淡寫
6. credit *n.* 功勞，讚美
7. react *v.* 反應
8. derogatory *adj.* 貶低的
9. remark *n.* 評論
10. humility *n.* 謙虛
11. receive *v.* 接受，收到
12. gratitude *n.* 感激
13. recognition *n.* 認可，承認
14. maintain *v.* 維持
15. morale *n.* 士氣
16. assure *v.* 確保
17. performance *n.* 表現

■ Reading Comprehension Check

According to the text you read, answer the following questions.

(　　) 1. What's the main theme of this article?

    (A) Companies should give recognition to their employees.

    (B) Accepting compliments is more difficult than giving them.

    (C) Accepting compliments is not culturally related.

    (D) People like accepting compliments more than giving them.

(　　) 2. What does the word "stroking" mean in the last paragraph?

    (A) It's a way to reject praise or positive feedback in the workplace.

    (B) It's a polite way to decline compliments from people who seldom compliment others.

    (C) It's a way to accept positive feedback when people give compliments to us.

    (D) It's a current form of mutual praise or positive feedback found in the workplace.

(　　) 3. How do Americans accept compliments?

    (A) They downplay compliments by giving the credit to someone or something else.

    (B) They decline compliments by recognizing the performance or work of others.

    (C) They regard a compliment as a great honor.

    (D) They give credit to others who may not be worthy of accepting compliments.

(　　) 4. In which area could this article most probably be found?

    (A) In musical studies.　　　　(B) In natural sciences.

    (C) In anthropological studies.　　(D) In cultural studies.

(　　) 5. The word "current" means "＿＿＿＿＿."

    (A) outdated　　(B) fashionable　(C) present　　(D) type

(　　) 6. When you compliment your American friend that her jacket looks great on her, she might ＿＿＿＿＿.

    (A) give the jacket to you

    (B) tell you that you can wear the jacket whenever you want

    (C) say that it's a cheap jacket and not worth praising

    (D) tell you that her sister choose it for her and she has a great taste for fashion

Expanding Vocabulary

Part A

Match the word on the right with the definitions on the left.

_____ 1. a sport instrument that people use for hitting balls

_____ 2. wonderful; extremely good

_____ 3. the quality of not deserving people's attention, respect, etc.

_____ 4. present, happening now

_____ 5. to express approval or admiration

_____ 6. to make certain; to ensure

_____ 7. to make something seem less important than it really is

_____ 8. the feeling of being grateful; thankfulness

_____ 9. showing a hostile or critical attitude

_____ 10. showing confidence and optimism

_____ 11. how well or badly a person does in an activity

_____ 12. the amount of positive feelings that people of a group have

_____ 13. likely to happen; possibly

_____ 14. to respond; to answer

A. derogatory
B. unworthiness
C. probably
D. racket
E. assure
F. performance
G. react
H. current
I. praise
J. fantastic
K. gratitude
L. morale
M. downplay
N. positive

Part B

Select the best answer to fill in the blank to complete each of the following sentences.

(   ) 1. He _____ the dancer on her skillful performance.
    (A) shrugged off   (B) complimented
    (C) downplayed   (D) reacted to

(   ) 2. My manager is late, and I guess he is _____ stuck in a traffic jam.
    (A) entirely   (B) actually   (C) thoroughly   (D) probably

(   ) 3. The traffic problem in the city is serious and it can't be _____ as if it doesn't exist.
    (A) reacted to   (B) referred to   (C) shrugged off   (D) pushed off

(   ) 4. You look _____ with your black silky hair and deep green dress.
    (A) frantic   (B) fascinated   (C) fragile   (D) fantastic

(   ) 5. The manager gave all his _____ to those who offered help.
    (A) strength   (B) belief   (C) credit   (D) trust

(   ) 6. The calm way in which you _____ to the stressful situation surprised me.
    (A) regretted   (B) referred   (C) regarded   (D) reacted

(   ) 7. A mean person always makes remarks that are highly _____.
    (A) incredible   (B) dispensable   (C) derogatory   (D) trustworthy

(   ) 8. My professor is a modest person. He always treats people with respect and _____.
    (A) humor   (B) humility   (C) humidity   (D) human

(   ) 9. The novel written in _____ of Hitler is banned by the government.
    (A) prize   (B) award   (C) praise   (D) rewards

(   )10. The company needs more _____ from consumers to improve their goods.
    (A) backpack   (B) washback   (C) cutback   (D) feedback

(   )11. My brother has a _____ attitude toward life.
    (A) repetitive   (B) relative   (C) positive   (D) selective

( )12. The government gave her an award in _____ of her contributions.
    (A) reception (B) institution (C) tuition (D) recognition

( )13. This news is good for boosting the baseball team's _____.
    (A) moral (B) morale (C) morality (D) mortal

( )14. The tickets to the music _____ next month at the National Concert Hall are sold out.
    (A) hall (B) tradition (C) preference (D) performance

( )15. Ever since he got a Ph.D, he has been _____ to as "Doctor."
    (A) shrugged (B) reacted (C) referred (D) responded

Part C

Match each of the following words or phrases written on the left with the proper definitions written on the right.

1. credit
2. humility
3. receive
4. maintain
5. remark
6. achievement
7. reward
8. shrug off
9. a pat on the back
10. give recognition to

(A) praise or recognition that one gives to others

(B) something one finishes successfully

(C) something one says to express what he or she thinks

(D) the quality of not being proud of oneself

(E) to have something given

(F) to treat something as unimportant

(G) to continue to have something or keep it in the same way

(H) praise or encouragement

(I) to give approval to the value of one's work

(J) something one gets for his or her good work or behavior

1. _____ 2. _____ 3. _____ 4. _____ 5. _____
6. _____ 7. _____ 8. _____ 9. _____ 10. _____

Part D

In the following you will learn three ways to derive a new word from the given word. Give the noun form for each of the following. Make changes if necessary.

Suffix "-ment"

Add the suffix "-ment" to the end of a verb to form a noun.

(1) achieve → *achieve**ment***

(2) treat → _____ (3) establish → _____

(4) accomplish → _____ (5) equip → _____

Suffix "-ance"

Add the suffix "-ance" to the end of a verb to form a noun.

(1) appear → *appear**ance***

(2) perform → _____ (3) disturb → _____

(4) accept → _____ (5) guide → _____

Suffix "-ness"

Add the suffix "-ness" to the end of an adjective to form a noun.

(1) worthy → *worth**iness***

(2) useful → _____ (3) happy → _____

(4) busy → _____ (5) lazy → _____

Part E

Complete each of the following by filling in one proper preposition in the blank.

1. Many people receive compliments from friends _____ gratitude.

2. We may try to shrug _____ the unfair comments made about us.

3. People from different cultures react _____ hugging differently.

4. The teacher gave rewards to students _____ their outstanding performance.

5. Shrugging your shoulders is usually referred _____ as refusing or denying.

6. I'd like to give compliments _____ Emily _____ her great achievement.

Part F

Select a proper phrase to complete each of the following sentences. Make changes if necessary.

give recognition to	refer to as	shrug...off
a pat on one's shoulder	unworthy of	compliment...on
give a reward to...for	receive...with gratitude	

1. Gambling is often _____ playing with fire.

2. He's an indulgent alcoholic and didn't take anyone's advice to quit. He is _____ our help.

3. The teacher gave me _____ when I got the first prize in the speech contest.

4. My boss _____ my hard work by giving me a raise.

5. All the guests who came to the party had a good time. They _____ the host and the hostess _____ the wonderful food and atmosphere tonight.

6. My mom _____ me _____ getting good grades in school. She bought a bike for me!

7. The food we eat everyday all comes from the efforts of many people. We should _____ it _____ .

8. James' coach complimented him on his excellent performance in the tennis match and he _____ it _____ with humility.

Speaking task

Conversation Practice

Invite a partner to practice the following conversation. Take turns to play part A and B.

A: You look so great today!

B: Oh, you mean this red dress? This is my sister's./You can say that again./Thank you.

A: This red dress really looks great on you.

B: It's the dress that looks great, not me./You made my day!/It's nice of you to say that.

A: Where did you get it?

B: From A & Z./It's my sister's and she bought it in Mexico./My mom made it.

A: You really have good taste in clothes./Your sister must be a very trendy person./Your mom is a wonderful tailor.

B: Thank you for the compliment./Yes, she is./Well, kind of.

■ Group Discussion

Form groups of four and discuss the following questions. Report your answers to the class.

1. When someone says "You did a wonderful job," how do you react to it?

2. According to the article, how do Americans react to compliments they receive?

3. When your friends tell you that you look good in your clothes, what do you say to them?

4. Look at the picture below. Discuss what compliments the man gives to the woman and what the woman says in response.

istening task

Part A

Listen to the CD carefully and answer the questions below.

(   ) 1. What is important in one's social life?

    (A) Having good social status.

    (B) Having a lot of money.

    (C) Giving compliments.

    (D) Giving condemnation.

(   ) 2. From this passage, we learn that giving praise is _____ receiving it.

    (A) easier than

    (B) harder than

    (C) the same as

    (D) more important than

(   ) 3. According to the CD, which of the following statements is correct?

    (A) People's attitudes to receiving compliments differ from culture to culture.

    (B) People all over the world react to compliments in the same way.

    (C) People like to be criticized more than complimented.

    (D) People don't like to give compliments to others.

(   ) 4. A second language learner should learn _____.

    (A) both cultural and linguistic knowledge

    (B) only cultural knowledge

    (C) only linguistic knowledge

    (D) either cultural or linguistic knowledge

(   ) 5. According to the recording, how do people react to compliments?

    (A) Americans react to compliments by learning a second language.

    (B) Chinese react to compliments by downplaying themselves.

    (C) Americans seldom contribute any credit to their friends.

    (D) Chinese people do not react to compliments properly.

6

Part B

Tom and Jerry are having a small talk with each other after a tennis game. Listen to their conversation on the CD, then answer the following questions.

1. Where did this conversation take place?
   It took place _____.

2. How did Jerry react to Tom's compliments?
   In the beginning, _____.
   At the end, _____.

3. Do you think Tom was complimenting Jerry? Why or why not?

   _____.

4. What may be Tom and Jerry's relationship?

   _____.

■ Error Correction

Look at the passage below. There are eight marked words or phrases. If the marked word or phrase is correct, put "C" in the blank. If not, put correct form in the blank.

Many Americans <u>shrugging off</u> compliments by <u>smiling</u>. Sometimes they
          (A)   (B)

<u>downplay</u> compliments <u>to give</u> the credit to someone or something
   (C)   (D)

<u>of others</u>. We know it is <u>easy</u> to give compliments than <u>to accepting</u> them.
   (E)   (F)   (G)

To learn <u>what</u> to accept compliments <u>is</u> important and necessary. It is
          (H)   (I)

<u>worthiness</u> <u>learning</u> how to <u>respond to compliments</u>.
      (J)   (K)   (L)

(A) _____   (B) _____   (C) _____   (D) _____

(E) _____   (F) _____   (G) _____   (H) _____

(I) _____   (J) _____   (K) _____   (L) _____

■ Translation

Translate each of the following Chinese sentences into English.

1. 他稱讚我的時候拍著我的肩膀。

   He ＿＿＿＿＿＿＿＿＿ when he ＿＿＿＿＿＿＿＿＿ me.

2. 她肯定我的網球技術。

   She gives me ＿＿＿＿＿＿＿＿＿ my tennis skills.

3. 老師讚美我們演出成功。

   Our teacher ＿＿＿＿＿＿＿＿＿ us ＿＿＿＿＿＿＿＿＿ our performance.

4. 愛迪生常常被稱為發明之父。

   Edison is often ＿＿＿＿＿＿＿＿＿ the father of invention.

5. 大部分新聞報導都對這次意外事件輕描淡寫帶過。

   Most news reports ＿＿＿＿＿＿＿＿＿ the accident.

6. 他對人生抱持著正面積極的態度。

   He has a ＿＿＿＿＿＿＿＿＿ toward life.

7. 我們需要消費者的回應意見以提高產品品質。

   We need consumers' ＿＿＿＿＿＿＿＿＿ to raise the ＿＿＿＿＿＿＿＿＿ of our products.

8. 他突如其來的對我大叫，我不知道該如何反應。

   All of a sudden, he yelled at me, and I don't know ＿＿＿＿＿＿＿＿＿.

9. 這是一個嚴重的問題，不能當作它不存在而置之不理。

   This is a serious problem and it can't be ＿＿＿＿＿＿＿＿＿ as if it doesn't exist.

10. 因為昨晚的精湛演出，我獲得許多稱讚。

    I ＿＿＿＿＿＿＿＿＿ because of the wonderful ＿＿＿＿＿＿＿＿＿ last night.

11. 我的老闆總是說出貶低別人的話。

    My boss always makes ＿＿＿＿＿＿＿＿＿ that are ＿＿＿＿＿＿＿＿＿.

12. 她永遠感激他的救命之恩。

    She felt eternal ＿＿＿＿＿＿＿＿＿ to him for saving her life.

13. 這個消息對提高全隊的士氣有好處。

    This news is good for boosting the team's ＿＿＿＿＿＿＿＿＿.

14. 他用謙虛的態度面對他的成就。

    He treated his ＿＿＿＿＿＿＿＿＿ with ＿＿＿＿＿＿＿＿＿.

∎Paragraph Development

Answer the following questions on the structure of the paragraph below.

Giving compliments is easier than receiving them. We can compliment others' achievements and beautiful appearance easily. We can find the right words to praise others without difficulty. But we always can't find the right words to react to the compliments given to us. For example, when people compliment us that our house is beautiful, we don't know what to say. Obviously, responding to others' compliment is more difficult than giving the compliment itself.

1. What is the topic sentence of the text?

2. How did the writer support this topic?
   ☐ By giving explanations.
   ☐ By giving examples.
   ☐ By showing a contrast.
3. The main idea of the paragraph is supported by one example. What is it?

Acknowledgments

Body Decoration

From Body Language-Codes and Ciphers-Communicating by Signs, Writing and Numbers. Published by Wayland (Publishers) Ltd. Reprinted by permission of the publisher.

Good Luck, Bad Luck

From Project Achievement: Reading B. © 1982 by Scholastic Inc. Reprinted by permission of Scholastic Inc.

Language in Clothes

From Body Language-Codes and Ciphers-Communicating by Signs, Writing and Numbers. Published by Wayland (Publishers) Ltd. Reprinted by permission of the publisher.

Animal Communication

From Body Language-Codes and Ciphers-Communicating by Signs, Writing and Numbers. Published by Wayland (Publishers) Ltd. Reprinted by permission of the publisher.

Take a Walk

From Project Achievement: Reading D. © 1984 by Scholastic Inc. Reprinted by permission of Scholastic Inc.

Accepting Compliments

From Communicator I by MOLINSKY/BLISS, © 1994. Reprinted by permission of Prentice-Hall, Inc., Upper Saddle River, NJ.

Photo Credits

All pictures in this publication are authorized for use by:
Dreamstime, FOTOLIA (picture on page 4: © Jiang Jingjie), iStockphoto, and ShutterStock.